# Oh My Gosh, Mrs. McNosh!

# Oh My Gosh, Mrs. McNosh!

by Sarah Weeks

pictures by Nadine Bernard Westcott

SCHOLASTIC INC.

New York  Toronto  London  Auckland  Sydney
Mexico City  New Delhi  Hong Kong  Buenos Aires

ISBN 0-439-56617-7

Text copyright © 2002 by Sarah Weeks
Illustrations copyright © 2002 by Nadine Bernard Westcott
All rights reserved. Published by Scholastic Inc.,
557 Broadway, New York, NY 10012,
by arrangement with Laura Geringer Books, an imprint of
HarperCollins Publishers.  SCHOLASTIC and associated logos are
trademarks and/or registered trademarks of Scholastic Inc.

12 11 10 9 8 7 6 5 4 3 2 1          3 4 5 6 7 8/0

Printed in the U.S.A          23

First Scholastic printing, October 2003

Typography by Jennifer Crilly

*For my country neighbors—*

*Malcolm, Vicky, Emery, and Rupert*

*—SW*

*To Ella and Stukely*

*—NBW*

Mrs. McNosh took a walk in the park.

Her dog saw a squirrel and started to bark.

"Stop barking! Stop pulling!" said Nelly McNosh.

But George wouldn't listen, and so—

# Oh, my gosh!

He zipped through the flowers
and skipped through the trees,
barking at bicycles, babies, and bees.

He dove and he wove right past Mrs. McNosh.

"I'll catch you!" cried Nelly.

But then—

The boat sprang a leak,

so George had to jump out.

"I'll catch you!" cried Nelly.

She caught . . .

a big trout.

He crashed through a wedding
and trashed the buffet.

"I'll catch you!" cried Nelly.

She caught . . .

the bouquet.

"Come back here right now," hollered Mrs. McNosh.

But George just kept running until—

# Oh, my gosh!

He bumped the plump umpire,
then jumped the stone wall.
"I'll catch you!" cried Nelly.
She caught . . .

a fly ball.

He danced and he pranced,
then he shook and he rolled.
"I'll catch you!" cried Nelly.
She caught . . .

a bad cold.

"That's it, I give up. I can't catch you, it's true.

I know when I'm licked.

I've been licked, George, by you."

So Nelly walked back to her house all alone,
and there on the porch she saw George's old bone.
"I wish he'd come back," sniffled Mrs. McNosh.
Then she opened the door and she cried—